About the Author

Dreena Collins is from the island of Jersey. She has published two collections, The Blue Hour and The Day I Nearly Drowned – contemporary short stories exploring challenges such as family break-up and loss. She has also been published in periodicals, magazines, on-line and in anthologies.

Dreena has been shortlisted and long-listed in several writing competitions, including the Bridport Prize.

http://dreenawriting.co.uk
facebook.com/dreenawriting
Instagram.com/dreenawriting
Twitter: @dreenac

ALSO BY
Dreena Collins

The Day I Nearly Drowned (Short Stories Vol. Two)

The Blue Hour (Short Stories Vol. One)

Foreword

Birds are a recurring (though unintentional) theme across several pieces in this collection – the fragility, grace and weightlessness of them came to mind repeatedly during the writing process.

These stories vary between two-hundred and sixty, to one-thousand words and therefore qualify as 'flash fiction'. I am delighted to find that flash fiction is on the rise. It is a distilled, intense form. When I first started writing short stories, they were between three and six thousand words. As time has gone on, I have deliberately slashed my word count, testing myself to 'write tight' and to fit as much power as possible into as few words as a I can. In doing so, I have become more experimental in my work – flash somehow gives the writer licence to break the rules and forces you to find a different way to express what you want to say.

I've been delighted to receive some positive reactions to this work: as well as having stories included in Reflex Press, Eyelands and Bath Flash Fiction Award anthologies, this collection also contains three stories long and shortlisted in the Flash500 competition, one shortlisted by Fish Publications, and others listed by Retreat West.

And as I always say: if you enjoy this collection, please leave a review for me. You have no idea the difference this can make.

Dreena Collins

Bird Wing
(and other stories)

A Flash Fiction Collection

First published in 2019

ISBN: 978-1-9993735-4-2

Cover design by Dreena Collins

Contents

Appendix – One Hundred Word Stories

Bird Wing

The night you left us, I stayed awake until the sky woke up. The light through the curtains was a fresh bruise, stirring from black, to blue, to grey. I sat on the floor of the lounge; a bottle of wine stood proud and cold on one side - our dog lay on the other.

Towards dawn, I recall, I tried not to blink - fearful sleep or tears would conquer me. I was a warrior. I would not give in.

I moved to the sofa a few nights later. It took several weeks to make it to the spare room. When I did, I stayed on my side of the bed – considered putting pillows on yours, creating a hump to dupe my body into rest. But it was cold, inanimate: an insult to your memory.

The loss of you was a tree-stump, to trip me, to wrong-foot me, at least once an hour. Even now this happens, daily - and I am falling again. Tumbling.

Even now.

It is startling how time moves on, regardless. The calendar is splintered; whole weeks, months heaped into piles of before and after. And yet days continue to come. One after another. More and more of them, since you have gone. Mounding, piling up until this new era threatens to topple over and consume the past: to swallow my befores.

Memories, once vivid, are like a broken bird wing in decay. A crumbling moth. But I hold onto them. I box them up. They are dusty but they are mine, ours, so I keep them safe, and I preserve them as best I can.

I have become more logical in the last few months, at least. Computered. Decisive. I know I need to sleep. I know I need to use rooms the intended way: I cannot be sick in the kitchen sink. I cannot write on the walls of your study. I cannot lie across the dining table, the carcass of a beached whale - or stand in the garden, drunk, at 4 a.m.

It is not helpful to do such things.

You would be proud of me. I have started showering; I sometimes wash my clothes. I leave the house. I sleep in our room again, and Toby forms a furry lump beside me. Warm. I am not sick in sinks. I do not scrawl on walls.

And at night, I place your pillows on the floor, so they can catch me – now, yes, even now - when I fall.

I Take the Number 14 Bus to Town to See Aunty Sandra

I take the number 14 bus to town to see Aunty Sandra. On the way in, I plot her death.

The bus lurches and its wipers slap the windscreen. At each stop, it slowly fills; I watch.

They do not move independently, these people. They do not turn their heads to the view. They do not smile, chatter, shift position. They sit in silence and bob up and down over pot-holes. They are rooted, heavy with mobile phones and apathy.

Not me.

I've made a plan. I'm going to take her pills and crush them into tea-leaves. Then I'll watch her drink. I'll take the pot, leave the pill packet by her side. I'll pour the leaves around the rose bush in my tiny back garden.

I close my eyes, and picture the rose bush withering and turning bitter over time, brown leaves crumbling to ash, dust, branches rotting. Druxy. Dying. Disintegrating from the inside out.

People think you should be kind to the elderly. But the elderly are just the young who stuck around. Old is not a synonym for nice.

Aunty Sandra is an utter bitch.

And not just now. Before, always. She was always this way. She's made my life hell, so she can go to hell. Today.

The bus pulls up at Jameston shopping precinct and pauses. The driver gets out a form, starts writing. You'd think they'd give them iPads by now.

Tablets.

I close my eyes. Some of my earliest memories include looking up at her nails, dirt wedged beneath, while she scolded me, and enjoyed it.

She used to force me to sit at the table until my food went cold and grey. She used to spit her words into my face. She used to drag me out of bed to wash my face. She used to make me jump in star jumps until I puked; saw stars.

She used to make me read aloud - so nervous I stumbled over even simple words, until they became a spiral of mistakes and criticism with my heart tremoring in time with her drumming fingers; wondering, watching - what would those hands do next?

The bus revs up: snippets of stories pop into my head. The wheels on the bus go ruined and ruined.

No. That's wrong. Do it again.

I think I can't - I think I can't - I think I can't.

Rotting from the inside out.

In my dream, I watch her die in snippets. Taking it in at once would burn. Glimpses, glances, gathering pieces of her death into a whole in my mind's-eye. The landscape of her body is covered in the folds of patterned nylon. A cobweb of drool falls from her mouth to her chest. She slips, she falls, she goes - and I walk into elysian fields, while she races into the abyss.

Slap.

The number 14 bus heaves away.

I clench my fingers together into a nest, and marvel at how innocent they are.

Geraldine the Powerful

No one had ever taught Geraldine to read and write. They thought that because it was hard for her, that she wouldn't want to. Or couldn't.

But hard doesn't mean impossible.

And sometimes things that are difficult are good: like learning to ride a bike. Or learning to say: 'Worcestershire Sauce'. Or how to boil a soft-boiled egg.

Geraldine liked all those things.

She didn't remember much about school - she knew that she had gone but had a feeling that it wasn't for very long. She was at home with mum as a child, she recalled. Mum taught her numbers while they made scones. The house filled with doughy cinnamon and squidgy sultanas and they ate them warm, with butter, while they counted the raisins. Geraldine usually won, because she always ate two.

Mum told her that different doesn't mean bad, it just means different. And one day she wouldn't have to worry about anything because she would have all the money she needed and someone could take care of her, if that's what she wanted. Or she could fall in love, get married, if that's what she wanted. If that's what she liked.

Remembering mum made her feel a calmness settle across her skin. A tingle. A prickle, but a good one: it was fresh and reminded her of damp grass in the morning. Or sea mist.

Geraldine liked sea mist.

Paul said she was too stupid to learn. That it would hurt her little head. That it would tire her out. Wouldn't be good for her. Would be a waste of time. So, when mum died, so suddenly, so young, the lessons came to an end. He started giving her sheets to do on her own, but they were too tricky. How can you do what they want, when you can't read the words?

And then he gave her pictures to colour. Lots and lots of pictures. She quite liked that – she remembered shading faces blue, trees yellow, the mud red, turning the sky purple. She was magical. Powerful. But Paul didn't like that. Told her she'd done it wrong.

So, then he gave her dot-to-dot books.

And then he gave her nothing.

Geraldine was too old for school now. He didn't give her dot-to-dots for Christmas. It was her job to make the boiled eggs and toast. To put the can of soup in the saucepan. Make it hot but not too hot.

Don't let it burn and stick to the saucepan, you fool.

Then take the plates from the table and stack the dishwasher. Carefully. Do it carefully.

Paul shouted even more these days, although she tried very hard to remember to wash the white clothes on their own and to make the coffee just right. To not leave her shoes, or his shoes, in the middle of the floor. She didn't like it when he shouted. She felt it in the skin on her face, like a scold. Geraldine didn't like that.

For the last couple of years, at night, Paul had been falling asleep on the sofa after too many bottles of beer. Geraldine would take the bottles and put them in the glass bin but leave the T.V. on because the change in sound, when she switched it off, could sometimes wake him, she found. She would sneak up to her room with his tablet cradled under her arm, and let it illuminate a tent of sheets as she tapped its screen, under the covers.

She had to remember to put it back before the morning. Geraldine always remembered.

At first, she had used it to watch cartoons, and funny videos of cats. Then a few weeks later she had started to play games. That was fun.

Then one night she discovered that if you spoke into it, sometimes it spoke back. It answered her questions. Incredible. And she found that she could listen to books too, listen to words, that it could read words. Read aloud, her words. And that she could write notes and messages.

She stayed up for hours, pressing things, trying things. Getting it wrong sometimes. She often got things wrong. But she carried on.

It was a bit hard. But that didn't mean it was bad.

Geraldine's skin tingled like it was covered in sea-salt. Magical. Powerful. She watched the dark light turn to bright light around her as she stayed awake until dawn. But she did not care.

In the morning, Paul was still lying on the sofa when she came down. He was rubbing the skin on his eyes, hard. He was circling his fingers in his eye sockets. He turned, eventually, towards her as she approached him. He let his arms fall, heavily, by his side.

"I need coffee," he said.

She didn't answer, and she walked towards him, still carrying his tablet. Bold. Brave. But he had not even noticed. All those times she had snuck back into his bedroom, or crept downstairs to put it in his bag, and he didn't even notice.

"What?" he snapped, when she stood still before him.

"I've been listening to my stories," she said.

"Good for you."

"I wrote a note for you," she said.

He snorted. "Right. Well. Coffee first."

"No," she said, "Read it now. Please read it now."

She could hear her voice, up high, tight, like a little girl. A child. And louder than usual.

Like a risk.

He started to sit up.

"What the –"

She shoved the tablet in front of his face. He pushed it away, irritated, as an unwanted cat. Something to swat. But she left it there; she didn't move.

"I did it," she said. "I did it."

He sat up fully and rubbed his eyes again, then he snatched the tablet from her.

"Very good, well done," he said, before he had even had time to read it.

But then she watched his face change as he read the words, and she watched her shape change before his eyes, and she imagined that she became Geraldine, different but good, different but powerful, as he read her note.

'This is my house,' it said. 'Get out.'

Dandelion Clock

Six days after Henry died, I climbed out of the bedroom window, jumped, and ran.

I remember grass on bare legs; pink sky; gossamer spiders' webs tangled across shoelaces; dandelion clocks fractured time into down, around my feet. The air was chill on my bed-sweated skin.

When I returned, days later, Mark's kiss was like a wet slap. I recall, clearly, the shock of it.

But I don't remember much in between.

Mark felt my departure as shame. He held me, made hot drinks - but he couldn't forgive me. My skin stretched taut as drumskin across swollen pupils when he ordered sleep; food tasted metallic; his milky tea made me retch.

He thought I was running from reality - but I was running from him. I wanted to buckle in, to curl around my hollow stomach. I wanted to lie, secret, alone, vomit as confetti around me. This was the correct response, I knew. But he wouldn't let me.

It was not long before I had lost a husband, also.

Now, the light outside the bedroom window is gun-metal grey; the grass is mud; the air is cooler still. I am alone in confetti. Gossamer spiders' webs trace puppet strings from the ceiling.

I lie here, periodically rising for milk-less tea and stale biscuits. I do not sleep.

I lie here, alone, within fractured time and space.

Except for a belly, swollen tight and taut, furtive, patterned, secret; a dandelion clock of possibilities, where a hollow stomach had once been.

These Things Did Not Happen to Us

It was 2 a.m. when the storm hit. I remember sitting on the edge of my windowsill, thrilled, electrified to be there - awake, with lights off and dad close by. These things did not happen to us.

The street was alive with a swarm of debris. The tree opposite was buckling: scrawny branches tattered as frayed ribbon. Random objects flew past, erratically – a carrier bag; a fractured umbrella; a tarpaulin. Periodically, something larger was lobbed, hurtling along as we screamed with joy and fear, unsure where it would come to rest. We saw a black bin-lid crash into a motorbike; corrugated metal fly into a van door.

Mum wondered where Mr English was, our neighbour. He'd gone out this evening, she said. His car was missing. He hadn't come back. I glanced at dad, saw him chewing the inside of his cheek, his familiar dimple, winking.

Around 3:30 a.m., the wind was placated. Hot chocolate gone, eyes heavy, mum persuaded us to go back to bed. No school tomorrow, she told us. Too many roads were blocked. Too many rooftops were damaged.

I woke at 8 a.m. They were downstairs, talking urgently.

"Oh!" cried mum, "Why are you awake?"

I didn't know how to answer so I said nothing.

"Love," dad said, "We can't find Tiger. He's been out all night."

"He's probably sheltering somewhere," mum interjected.

"Yeah."

"OK," I said. But I felt weird.

Mum went to the window and opened the curtains. She peered, frustrated, then opened the latch, and a blast of wind broke into the room as she tried to see further, see more.

"Your friend not back?" Dad asked. He said the word 'friend' in a funny voice; I didn't like it.

She shut the window.

"I'm going to look," she said.

"Is she going to get Tiger?" I asked. Dad stood straight; he was tense, taut, with little muscles and tendons flickering in his arms. He didn't answer me.

Mum went outside wearing pyjamas, with wellies, a coat. When she opened the front door, I saw fat raindrops hammering into puddles, breaking the surface as bubbling soup. Dad was watching, chewing his cheek, his dimple bulging and shrinking.

I wasn't allowed to go with her.

I sat at the table and drew – pictures of trees distorted, winded. Pictures of damaged cars, of cats, families.

Mum came home a long time later - Tiger in her arms. He was wet. But he was fine, mum said. Fine. So I didn't know why she was crying.

I sat on a chair and she placed him into my lap, enfolded him in a towel. I curled around him, drying, preening, and mum wrapped her arms across both of us. We sat still together in a cocoon as they both shivered into a new warmth. We sat still and centred, as a vortex; as an eye.

Still; until a swift, unexpected wind ran through the house when a door opened and closed again - and my dad was gone.

Friends

He is looking at your account, and your comments and your profile. You haven't seen him in years. He hasn't seen you in years and he has changed but you have not. You are tea and biscuits comfort – familiarity. A welcome face.

JonathonJones appreciates the opportunity to get back in touch with a long-lost friend. This is a wonder of the modern world; how marvellous that we can find each other at the click of a button. The flick of a switch.

He is looking at your business, and your photos and your family; your baby on the day it was born. How lovely. Its body. Its skin. It is wrinkled and wriggling as a pink, bald mouse. He does not say this, of course. Like an appendage of yours, attached to your chest in a vacuum, he does not say.

JonathonJones does not have a baby. Or a business. Or a yours.

He is trawling through your memories, your histories, your yesterdays. Do you remember? Your history? It was blushing, fledgling, fragrant. It was heady - it was. Until it exploded into particles. Shattered. Splintered. Smashed.

Good times.

LOL.

He is surprised to see you with your father. He had thought him long gone. Disappointing, really. But how well he looks, he says - with semi-colons, twitching like squashed ants.

He is calling your name, softly. He is tracking, trawling, watching your page. Liking you.

JonathonJones loves this. He does.

He is trawling, crawling, and your words fly through the page like starlings at sunset. Swooping. Swarming. Black lines. Blackness. Into the dark.

Click, click, flick. He flicks.

JonathonJones remembers you well. Remembers it all. JonathonJones shared this.

He checks which friends are not his friends. None of them are. He checks which ones need reporting. Deporting. He knows them now; he did not know them. He knows their type. He knows what they like.

He is looking at your account, and your comments and your profile. And your car. And your house.

Your front door.

You haven't seen him in years. He hadn't seen you in years and he has changed but you have not. You are fresh and confusing – familiarity and chaos and he is falling down and back, with arms outstretched and open and tumbling, sinking, shattered - falling down into images. Photos. Scenes.

Into the blue.

Click, click, flick.

JonathonJones has started following you.

Ruby

She decided to wear a ruby red scarf with the black dress. Sod it.

Robert didn't like red. Or scarves. But then she wasn't asking him to wear it now, was she?

The bright chiffon seemed to emphasise her paleness, picked up on the two little spots on her chin. But it also looked striking. And whimsical. Free.

"Oh," he said, when he saw her, "Wow."

But he said it like it meant 'Yuck,' or 'Ugh', or 'Holy hell.'

"Are you ready?" she asked, chirpily, ignoring this.

He said nothing and picked up the keys that hung, so orderly, from their hook by the front door. The hallway was grey, matched his trousers, she noticed.

Outside, it was cool, but the autumn sun was attempting to fight back. It dappled through the trees; winced into their eyes.

She grabbed his arm.

"Let's walk!" she cried, as if this was the most scandalous thing she could suggest. He frowned, paused, placed the keys in his trouser pocket while holding her gaze.

They started to march, a brisk pace. She felt the red chiffon building friction and sweat against her neck. She was determined to ignore it.

"I don't know why we don't walk into town more often!" she said.

"Because the night bus home is hideous?" he muttered. She could hear his keys jingle as he stepped. Out of place. She took his hand. It sat limp in hers, damp and warm like a dirty flannel.

"We could walk back, too?"

"If we fancy being mugged, then yes, we could," he replied. She ignored this.

They arrived at the pub, pushed the door open to a wall of heat and noise. A gambling machine flashed neon, directly ahead. They had lit the fire, quite unnecessarily, and it crackled to their left. Kim and Ben weren't there yet so they decided on a table in the corner, far right.

Robert took off his coat, reached one arm out. She was confused, wasn't sure what he wanted. She placed her hand in his. They stood still for a moment. She could feel pink heat rising her cheeks.

"Scarf?" he said, simply.

She dropped his hand, pictured a dank hand-towel falling to the table with a slap.

"Oh, I'm going to keep it on," she replied. He raised one eyebrow and walked towards the bar.

She turned the scarf a little, spun it around like a cloth in a dance, then faster. A whirligig. It was addictive once she had started.

"Gin and tonic?" he stated - as he walked away.

She waved the scarf before her face, marvelling at the shades and shape and texture. Then she lay it across her lap, spread out thin, square - a safety net.

"I'll have red wine," she called after him as he left. He stopped for just a moment, and his head jolted on his neck, and as he did so she felt something that she could not ignore: a glimmer of something, sparkling in her belly.

Mr Harrison and the Unknown

It makes him sad, Mr Harrison says, that people don't have respect for their country anymore.

It hurts me, lad.

He says this when he realises someone has stolen the Union Flag and the England Flag from their little stand outside the shop door.

Is the Confederate Flag gone, too? I ask.

He nods his head, and his jowls rock, and I can smell the air around him turn beefy as he sighs. He is like a tired puppy. A baby Bulldog. And although he is a big man, and old, for a moment I do feel sorry for him.

It's like the time they stole his MAGA hat, he says. That was a sad day, lad. That one hurt bad. I brought that all the way back from the U.S of A, you know - he says.

Mr Harrison pats the shop counter, with its wood worn down like happy memories, into a nothing, into something else. He pats the counter where his hat was, as if to conjure it back again. It's so disappointing, he tells me. It bruises my very soul, he says.

But you're a good boy, he states, and leans in, to ruffle my hair. I step back. You're not like them. You understand. You respect queen and country, he tells me. He knows that.

He stops. Did I deliver those leaflets when I did the papers? All of them?

I got rid of them all, Mr Harrison, I say.

And he smiles a watery smile and stares at the poster on the wall, then the poster in the window, where a white man looks like a pink man and shouts angry statistics in capitalised, red letters. So sad that we have to do this, Mr Harrison says.

And later, when I am home, and warm, and clean, I will think again of what a good lad I am. I will remember his words as I open the drawer by the side of my bed. A baseball cap. A bunch of leaflets. Three little flags. I will think of Mr Harrison – so very sad - and how what he doesn't know, won't hurt him.

Saying Yes

They pushed the little boat from the shore of the lake to clamber aboard. He held it steady for her as it tried to tip and topple. She giggled. They were no experts, but he stood sturdy, firm, even as he lifted the cool-bag from across his shoulders and dumped it, one handed into the boat. He had water to his knees.

Ready? He asked. Yes, she was.

They began the slow and gentle journey to the middle, tracking their path by the sun that hung low in the sky. The clouds and the air were auburn now. The lake reflecting back the sunset. Burnt orange water.

After a while, he noticed her begin to flag - tired, or simply bored perhaps. He suggested they rest and enjoy the view. Eat something. Drink something. She turned her head to look at him, smiled, excited. Yes.

He rose cautiously and turned his back to her, bent over the bag. He stood with feet apart, legs a solid V, bending forward in the half-light to find a bottle of red wine. Did she want some of this? He asked. Yes. Yes, she did.

She took the wine and held it firm between her knees as she began to unpeel the foil around its neck.

He returned to his rummaging in the bag. Little boxes, parcels, packages, treasures. Fruit. Cheese. He was absorbed, choosing.

"Who is Kayleigh?" she asked.

He stopped moving, stayed bent over, didn't turn, didn't reply.

They both remained still except for the gentle rocking of the little boat on the orange water.

One beat. Two beats. Three.

Then she stood too, and the boat lilted. She lifted the bottle with both hands, high, not quite above her head, almost above her head, and she smashed it across the back of his skull. She smashed it and the red wine mixed with red blood, sprayed into the brown and orange water. He staggered, then fell, toppled heavily into the lake, dazed.

He burst up in the water, gulping, flopping, inept. The blood thinned and spread across his face as it hit the lake. The water around him slapping, dipping the little boat on miniature, sudden waves.

"Help me," he spluttered.

She noticed the foil had sliced into her fingers, sprayed the floor in ant specks, blood and red wine had splattered, painting the orange boat a new red in places.

"No," she said.

And she picked up the oars.

Nimbus

I had never been in a wooden house before. Our house was glass, metal, tile. Cold things, harsh things. Hard. This place was elemental and crumbling and warm. Walls and roof a continuum of planks.

The sky above was a many coloured thing. A sea of midnight blue, turquoise - even black - by day. A blanket freckled with white by night.

The sky at home was always ash grey.

I had never really been in the countryside before. At least not like this. But Mum had sent me on a summer school of sorts – an adventure in long grass and pollen and oxygen. I did not fare well at first, with my patent shoes and keyboard skills. These things hold no value in fields.

By summer's end my pointed shoes had been replaced with Ned's old wellies, too big, too old, cracked - perfect.

The next year, my feet were prepared. My hands made daisy chains and camp-fires. I lay on my back as quick fingers split flower stems like green beans, watched the clouds trundle past me, wondered when they would give up and dissolve into the milkiness seen at home.

After that, I brought binoculars. Shelf clouds, mushrooms, stratocumulus. Ned stared at me in fascination as I listed them all: did not want the binoculars that I tried to share, wanted instead to stare at my face, my mouth, as I said the peculiar words.

In spite of the beautiful blots in the sky, my windswept skin was tanned by summer's end.

And then we were back again, and the house was there, and the clouds were there, but he was only half there; careworn and distant among the bees and the grass. New black boots harsh against the pale skin of his shins. Sometimes he stared at my face as I spoke. Sometimes he touched my cheek. Sometimes he stared at the clouds, alone, while I cut holes in the stems of daisies and waited for childhood to return. Nimbus clouds warned us of rain, I told him.

Our house was glass, metal, tile. Cold things, harsh things. Hard. This place was elemental and crumbling and warm. Walls and roof a continuum of planks and so nature took its course, and the following year I could not go to visit my clouds. I could not go to see my grass, my flowers, my Ned. The roof was leaking, they said. They would replace it with tar or tiles, I thought, no doubt.

I pictured holes in the ceiling, I imagined lying in bed with fractured glimpses of innocent sky, and stars, and cirrus - high up, wispy and light, poking through the cracks.

But the sky at home was always ash grey.

Picture This

Daddy has turned his neck to muscle. Where bristle and worm skin usually rests, there are ropes and strings.

He is sitting opposite Mrs L-D. There is a desk between them. On his face he has placed a very serious look – one I had only seen on him rarely.

Like the time Jonny took that bike from two doors down and everyone thought they might call the Police. He used that face on Mrs Stephens. I remember how she stood in our doorway, holding the bike in a peculiar way, one handed, firm, high, staring at the floor - pink faced.

Daddy looked at her the same way as he is looking at Mrs L-D.

Mrs L-D has placed my drawing on the desk. She keeps tapping it as she talks.

"You can see why I would be concerned," she is saying. "I hope you understand why I had to ask you in."

It's the picture I did about Jeni. About the secret.

Mum stands by the corner of the desk. She places one hand on daddy's shoulder, but he doesn't respond, so she lets it drop again. There isn't another human sized chair in the room. She leans over and swizzles the picture around to face her.

"Children do draw peculiar things, sometimes," she says.

Mrs L-D says nothing. She taps the place where the picture was, where she thinks the picture should be, and stares at the desk.

"Miss Daniels will be here shortly," she tells us, "she was called away for an urgent issue."

Miss Daniels is important. I don't know exactly what her job is, but I do know that I don't want her to be here. In this room. With too many grown-ups, not enough chairs. I start to feel a little patch of lumpy sick forming in my stomach.

I don't want to be in trouble.

There is a long pause. Daddy swings his right leg, like he's trying to be relaxed, but it's just a little bit too fast. Just a little bit too wide. He bangs the table a couple of times with the tip of his shoe, and then he stops.

Miss Daniels comes in. Mum looks like she wants to shake her hand, but she has a notebook and a tablet in her arms, and she doesn't try to move them out the way. She does a strange little smile at mum and then nods at Mrs L-D.

"Sorry about that – data crisis," she says, as if we will know what she means, "I assume Mrs Lederer has brought you up to speed with our concerns."

Mrs Lederer. Ledrerer. Lerderer. Ledrerer. I try to roll the beats of the word around in my mouth, but they are bumpy and wrong.

"Concerns?" daddy says, in a sort of snorty way. His serious face is changing into an angry face, I notice. There is a little patch around his eyes, where the colour doesn't match the rest of his face. Mum touches his shoulder again.

"Why do you think she would have drawn such a picture?" Mrs Daniels says.

"Why don't you try asking her yourself?" Daddy answers.

"We did," says Mrs L-D, "but she wouldn't say."

"Wouldn't?" Mum asks, quickly, "Or couldn't? Didn't know, I mean."

I am very proud that I have kept the secret.

Miss Daniels starts talking in a quieter voice and explaining something about passing this sort of information on and it's always important to follow things up. Not to take any risks when it comes to safety. All the time she is looking at me and then down to the picture. Flicking her eyes between the two.

"I really think she should be waiting outside," she states.

Daddy turns around to me, full. He drops his foot to the floor, and I can see him try to make his face look gentle, but the string and the pink bits are still there, underneath and around the soft parts of his face.

"Darling," he says, "You aren't in trouble. Just tell us why you drew the picture. Even if it was just for fun. Was it just for fun? Experimenting?"

"Um, I really don't feel comfortable with this type of –" Miss Daniels tries to interrupt him, but he is in full flow.

"Is that what it is? Just a silly little thing? Did it come from nowhere? Or was it a cartoon perhaps. Did you see something like that on T.V.?"

If I get Jeni in trouble, she will be angry with me. She won't be my friend anymore. And she will tell everyone I am a liar. She told me so. Lots of times.

I can feel the lumpy sick moving higher now, into the back of my throat. I pull my cardigan sleeves down and pinch them into the palms of my hands, imagining the row of nails along my skin, indented like teeth marks.

I look down, shake my head. He flops back in his chair, frustrated, angry, sad, I think. But I can't tell him. I can't.

Because it's not my secret to tell.

Mother's Day

British Summer Time begins, and we spring towards fresh-cut grass, dew sodden mornings, daffodils. Clocks losing time yet hours somehow extending. Amongst the nature and the numbers nestles Mother's Day. And you are not here.

April Fool's Day: yes, this suits. A fool to let you go, when you were taken. Though I should have done better. Been better.

Good Friday, and almost a month more has fallen past me, slipped through my arms, dissolving and disintegrating into motes of dust. Not good, gone. You left. No: were taken. And I know I should have done a better job. And I know I should have tried harder. But it was hard, my love. It was hard.

Easter Sunday is here: with richness and its micro-Christmasness. You loved it when I left a trail of miniature eggs to track. Crack. Chocolate and foil and joy, with a basket or bowl to capture them. To take. I did not do this last year, that's true. Or the one before, no. But I would have done it now; I would have tried. Hard.

Easter Monday and people are off work and I am off work because I am always off work. I would have sat with you and watched a film, if I could. I would have made sure you had some clothes to wear this time. I promise. Real clothes. I would have kept you safe, wrapped and happy, but you have gone so I cannot. It is hard, my love. You are not here.

May Day, and it is almost summer. I can feel the warmth attempt to infiltrate my bones. You would have liked that. You liked to be warm. Don't. No. I am sorry, love. I should have listened. And people are off work and I am off work because I am always off work and I cannot remember the last time I did or the last time I saw you but I am trying. I am.

Though they say it is too late.

Father's Day and you leap into his arms. I picture you; see it. You love him now. You know him: time enough has passed and so you leap into his arms and through my arms and I am alone, a fool. I am dissolving into atoms, tumbling apart; I am crumbling paper, powder, ash - with specks of dust, and loss, and disintegration.

The Painting

"I'm going to buy that painting," he told her. "One day, I'll buy it for you."

He was good at making promises.

She squeezed his hand quickly, twice, and glanced up at him. She had one of those warm half-smiles on her face, that she so often had. It was the reason strangers spoke to her first, not him. The reason babies did not cry. People opened doors.

For three years, they visited the same gallery on holiday, in the same week, of the same month.

"Let's go to see my painting," she would say. And they would stand and look with their two squeezed hand-holding and half smiles, and promises.

But then the next year he was too busy for a holiday. They would go the following year, he said. Or soon. They would go. She could count on him.

She gave a half-smile but a different half-smile. She gave him the other half.

And when they did go back, eventually, it was after six years. In a different month.

"See, I always keep my promises," he said, as he checked his messages, fiddled with his phone.

But it was gone. Her painting, their gallery.

And it was gone altogether, her smile, as she gave his hand a squeeze – just the once – before she let it go.

It Was Never There

Many years ago, she had lost it. She hadn't known at the time that she might not find it again. Careless, she was; just a teenager.

It was sweet and lovely, hard to quantify. Plastic, fragile, delicate. A wren's egg of a thing.

Then there was a space where it should be.

Periodically, she looked for it. She found similar things, sometimes: an echo of what she had lost; cosy, familiar but mundane against the sharpness of her one lost, perfect thing. They were plum jam comfort. Knit-one, Pearl-one. She wanted sour lemons, sparkles, tangerines.

She kept searching. Desperate sometimes; foolish, perhaps. People said her memory tricked her. It was only a thing, an artificial thing. And she had no witness. So, they wouldn't believe. Would not believe her.

But still she looked: ransacking, ravaging boxes, spaces, sometimes. A jumble of bags and blankets; empty vessels.

It was never there.

Until yes, one day, she heard its familiar humming; felt popping candy on her skin, mouth, ears.

It was in a place she had never thought to look, her lovely thing. She worked, lifted layers and mounds, dust, damp cloth, refuge - until it was revealed. A peacock. A wren's egg.

A tangerine.

She looked down to her hand, her fingers – herself - splattered in dirt, memories. Tentatively, she reached out. One hand out, skin brushing feathers, light, bright, lemons. Touching now, tingling, ready to hold on. She was ready.

Hold on.

Grasping, clutching - for a moment thinking this was not quite what she expected. Not quite what she wanted. Not quite.

No.

But it must be. It must. She only needed this.

And so, she persisted. She tried. She pushed through and on and she looked down to her hand, to her fingers, nails. Lines on her palm an atlas, coordinates, trails.

Then she held it aloft, and she stared, and she wondered, as dispersing, dissolving – she disappeared.

Gathered with the Birds

Gathered with the birds, we squash the dew into our socks, and wait for sunrise.

The sky is covered in the misty smear that you only see in half-light. It hangs too low over the fields. Pretty, but ominous, I think.

I am just a little scared.

We had to get up early, either way. Why not watch the sunrise, too, you said? I couldn't think of any nots; though lots and lots of whys.

You wanted to see this before you left. You wanted us to wake, together, with the birds and the trees and the too-low sky.

Magical, you say. This is real air. Both real and make-believe, I think. Like hope. A dream but much too real, I do not say.

The air is gathering into puffs around us as you talk, as you describe it to me, you tell me what we see. I swallow it up, the best of you, gulping breath and language until it fills my mouth too far. It clogs. But tell me, tell me more.

You wanted to see this before you left - the plane, the plans, they pull us forward into mid-morning coffee and civilisation. I close my eyes and hope the sky stays so low that it does not let you leave. I want to listen to you tell me what we see. I want to stay, standing on wet grass, smeared, where I am scared, just a little.

In the dew, amongst the birds, clouded in hope: before you leave.

The Bloated Fish

She offered no explanation for the black eye, and I did not ask. She had arrived late – hair flopping down in a visual rebuttal of questions, concerns.

"Oh," I said, shocked; clumsy. "Wow!"

"It's not as bad as it looks," she replied.

Then she put the post and a coffee on my desk and walked away.

That day, whenever I saw her, I was unsettled. I should ask - I knew I should ask. Instead, through a string of platitudes and instructions, I gulped my words and avoided any acknowledgement of the obvious; I panted them out like a grey and stranded fish, leaving no air between us, just lumpen, bloated sounds. I was desperate to ensure there was no room for embarrassment, shame.

And yet at the same time, that was all there it was.

She brought in my afternoon coffee. I kept my eyes on the computer, squinting: shifting the world into a blur, her image into a haze.

Five o'clock came and she left, and I wondered where she had gone to – what she had gone to.

Frustrated, ashamed, I sat and searched the internet, quickly, urgently - pressed print. I grabbed it and highlighted: the number of the refuge, hotlines, advice. I circled and slashed: angry at what had happened – at what I had not done.

I left a nameless envelop on her chair and went home.

The next day, I came in early: twitchy, almost excited. I wanted her to see what I had done. I wanted her to know.

But while the morning woke up, she did not arrive, or call - contacted no one. And as time passed and afternoon approached, the grey fish bloated in my stomach, filling the space where the coffee would sit with nausea, and fear, and lost opportunities.

Itch

Sepia, black, grey clothes. Trousers, jumpers mostly. Her world was lacking colour.

There was nothing much in here that would be suitable for a date.

She flicked through the hangers, clothes sliding off metal shoulders, slipping to the floor of the closet. She didn't stop. It wasn't as if any of it was precious.

Her fingertips flicked between acrylic and wool, tingling with a suppressed itch. She settled on a black jumper and slim-fitting trousers but added a flash of colour in a scarf. A red scarf, with a pattern that could be mistaken for roses, but was in fact a sea of day-of-the-dead sculls. Inappropriate? Perhaps.

She went downstairs, poured herself a bottle of beer to settle her nerves, enjoyed watching the mist of condensation cover the thin glass. She took a long swig, and then rummaged in her bag for her iPod to find some music to accompany her as she finished getting ready.

She had been so shocked when she had seen him, standing in front her, still with that boyish grin. How long had it been? She had hardly seen him since school, except the odd photograph on social media, posted by friends of friends, and that one time when she had seen him briefly in La Siesta, when he was back in town to visit his sister.

But he still looked the same.

On the edge of the bed, she made herself comfortable and then turned the mirror on the chest of drawers around, to face her. It was a small mirror, mottled. It speckled her face with brown spots and ripples around the edges. But its image was slightly soft with age, and grease, she supposed. She liked it that way.

She considered her red lipstick, but quickly dismissed it. Not too much make-up, she decided. No. She didn't want him to think she was too keen. Plus, it was important not to be uncomfortable. Most days she barely wore make-up at all; it would be strange to do so tonight.

She rummaged at the bottom of the wardrobe for her black Louboutin's. She didn't have many occasions to wear high-heels so this concession was worth it, and worth the ache in her legs she would have the next day.

He'd be here soon.

She slugged down the rest of the beer, enjoying the cold tear of it pouring down her gullet towards her empty stomach. A quick tidy of her bedroom, she turned the iPod off and then tottered carefully down the stairs.

She was just checking herself in the full-length mirror - somewhat aghast at the swell of her belly under her trousers and jumper, the little roll above the waist band - when the doorbell rang. Too late to back out now.

She went into the hallway, took a breath, then opened the front door. And there he was.

Edwin.

Beige raincoat, grey suit, plain wooden walking stick. His grey, receding hair was thin now, but carefully swept back into his trademark quiff. His face was furrowed with delicate, papery lines, crinkled by love, age.

His face filled with his boyish grin.

"You haven't changed a bit," he said, softly.

At Night She Came Alive

At night she came alive. Feet clipping on paving slabs, heart pounding in chest and ears. Blood pumping. Exhilaration. Joy.

Fear.

Alone, she slung her rucksack over one shoulder. Khaki, tatty, no doubt it had never been near an army-store - but it transformed her into a warrior.

At The Rose and Crown she made her way to the toilets. There were girls in there, so she went into a cubicle and removed her scarf, gloves, pulled off her jumper. She zipped up ankle boots, their chains, little beads, falling down and across the arch of her foot as a string of teeth.

She waited until she heard them leave: a little flock patting, preening, fluttering around each other. The door swung behind them, the noise of the bar briefly entering, lost, entering again, until it closed.

She came out into the space, took out her washbag. Wax in hair, lipstick almost black – not quite black – more eyeliner, more blusher, more everything. Bracelets on wrists; her favourite ring. Transfiguration.

Back out through the bar and she pushed past the dancers wobbling, jiggling in a damaged swarm. A man, around 40, stared as she approached. He didn't turn away as she squeezed through, and then winked, slowly. Her stomach lurched.

Outside, she walked with purpose towards the club: the wet pavement was a challenge now; the air cold in her thinner clothes. Rain. The illumination of street lights, shop lights, Chinese restaurants, etched the air in flashes. Head down, she felt that familiar feeling of guilt, but she stepped through it, walked faster.

As she approached the club, she placed gum in her mouth, spritzed her wrists. She said her name aloud.

"Eve," she said, over and over. Until it was true. Until the word consumed her whole.

"I am Eve."

Something About Bats

She said that she cared more about animals than she did about people, these days. She said this across the top of a coffee mug, eyes steamed up with froth and memories.

Timmy was fourteen now - old in cat years - and he needed a special diet and frequent vet visits. He was grumpy, inconsistent.

Much like I am, she said.

She said that she was volunteering now. Something about bats. Too many trees cut down; a travesty.

She squeezed her eyelids into narrow slits. A new tattoo was on her inner wrist, I noticed, as her sleeve rode up: a black fish.

Some days I speak to no one but my pets, she said. And I'm O.K with that.

They don't answer back, I quipped. Didn't know what else to say.

Actually, they do - in their way - she said, into the distance. She was turned around, looking for a waitress, one hand raised high. I shifted in my chair; tried to feel comfortable. Winced. Wanted to say more.

I have to go, she told me. I have commitments this afternoon. This raised more questions than it answered - but I didn't ask.

I have commitments too, I said. The hospital this afternoon.

She turned to look at me, but she kept her hand raised. A stop sign. Her eyes narrowed again, but she only said oh, she was sorry.

We shouldn't leave it so long, next time, I said. Let's make an effort. I made eye contact, rubbed my abdomen. And then she smiled, hand raised, eyes tight; nodded quickly.

She cared more about animals than humans these days, she told me.

And I was O.K with that.

She stood, and I watched her leave - waited a moment for the spasm of pain to pass.

Grief Had Her Foot on My Neck

Grief had her foot on my neck and would not let me swallow. She would not let me breathe more than tight, little bird breaths – no, moth breaths. I was shedding pounds and oxygen by the hour.

It was thirty-five days since it happened. People had stopped mentioning you, I had noticed - as if loss was a time-bound thing to be over within a month, and time was the antidote to loss. But it was the very cause.

So, I was sat in my car again, outside where you used to live. It was physically painful to look up. Each time I tried, a headache swamped my eyes: a sheet of white fell down from above.

On a previous visit, at my lowest, I had felt compelled, determined, and I had lifted my neck nonetheless, to stare into the piercing sunshine and up, up to your window - until I had retched, heaving a mound of heavy vomit into the footwell. I could still smell it now, sometimes.

Grief was a filthy liar, I had learned.

Instead, these days, I dialled your number; put it on speakerphone, waiting, urging you to answer. It rang out, rang off, of course. You were not there. I rested my head against the steering wheel.

"I miss you," I said aloud. An odd voice, dark: mine but bruised by tears.

I scrolled through our texts again, until the tiny letters flew up in a stream like bats from a cave. Hundreds, perhaps thousands of them. From you. To you. I tapped out another text: the only way I could think of to talk to you now.

Suddenly, my phone pinged. I jumped; a shrill jolt.

A text.

This is Michelle's boyfriend, Steve. Stop hassling her or we'll go to the Police.

Take-Away

Gran looks at Mum like she'll eat her alive.

"Two times seven is fourteen," I state. I don't know what else to say.

They stare at each other: blink one, pause one.

"I'll write it down, shall I?" mum asks.

She fetches the little notepad from next to the phone. The short wooden pencil digs hard into the paper, too hard, while she writes: '2, 7, 1 (Prawn Crackers), 29'. I picture the numbers indented into the sheets beneath, slowly fading through the pages until they disappear, like the trail of a sparkler, bubbles, butter in crumpet holes.

"Don't see why we can't share," says Gran, "Can't we share a boiled rice?"

She leans over to the menu and opens a flap with a flourish: big armed, wide handed, like it's a hardback book. Her thin wrists jangle with bracelets, charms falling onto the table as low-hanging fruit.

"See," she says, jabbing, "26. Boiled rice."

She juts out her chin. Mum tucks hers in.

"Half of twenty-six is thirteen," I say, quietly.

"Put on thirteen pounds in one sitting if you eat all that."

Gran harrumphs a sort of chuckle. But it doesn't sound funny and she's not really laughing.

"I'm hungry," mum says, "I am not sharing."

She speaks in a funny voice - like she doesn't have any air. I take a deep breath to fill my tummy; can't help myself. Gran shoots me a look, shoots my tummy a look. I suck it in.

She takes her black bag from the back of the chair and rummages for her purse. She counts out coins into her hand, one at a time, holding them up, each one, calculating.

Then she takes the notepad and writes: 'vegetable stir-fry (plain) - boiled rice'.

She doesn't add any numbers.

Shades of Grey

Down and around and down I go: into the dark. Into the hole. I am grappling, struggling, balancing here, lost in grey. I don't understand why you won't help me, why no one will help, no one can see. I'm falling.

They are oblivious, these people. They are hands-in-pocket people. Rocking-on-feet, whistling people. They are calibrated, calm, working people, going about their lives - while I am here and tumbling, before their eyes.

It is getting darker, danker. Quiet, except the scutter of the grit against my hands. Fingertips.

As I move, there is a backdrop of other people's blankets and dreams, blocking my sounds, my view. Stifling. Muffling. I don't understand.

Down and around, and I am falling deeper, going too far, I think. Perhaps I will not come back this time. I don't think I can.

It is blue grey, brown grey, cold grey here.

But you are useless, do nothing to help - your trite suggestions, shouted vaguely from afar. Sod you, shut it. Shut. No. Stop. Patronising, standing by, idly watching: thumb twitching, eye flinching. I don't want you. You do nothing; this means nothing. You, with the good life. Walking away.

It must be nice to be you.

Wait, no.

Please don't leave.

Down and around and down I go and into the dark I fall, I plummet, and I am almost gone. The rocks and shale and stones cascade beside me, a waterfall. Rapids. Rapid stone. Falling faster now.

I am calling you, calling, but you don't hear. Please. Come. I need you. Why won't you help? I am useless, that's why. A parasite, a tape worm. A heartworm. I am.

Quick, too quick. Useless. Scared.

And down and around and inside and slipping and my feet give way and I am losing and lost. Where are you? Where am I? But you hate me, you hate me, you must hate me. You must.

I am down, way down, over my head in the dark, with the rubble and stumbles and scutters and cold grey and pale grey and blue grey and brown grey.

And slate grey.

And black. And gone.

The Market

She was in the market, when I called. Buying fruit and veg. No matter, she said. She could talk.

The clatter of the people, the chatter, the colours floated behind her words like birdsong. Vibrant. Far away.

I sat on the edge of my bed, hugging a plugged-in mobile phone with a too-short battery life.

We had never spoken before. Her voice wasn't what I had expected, though at the same time, I knew it wouldn't be. Voices rarely match faces, I find. Hers was deep, bruised. Her face light, open, smiling always. In pictures, that is. It seemed to be.

"Are you sure?" I asked, hoping she might say no. Hoping it might give me a chance to bottle out.

"Of course!" she chuckled, grittily, "I'm an excellent multi-tasker."

Somehow, I took this as flirtatious, though I didn't know exactly what she meant. I shifted position, stared at the wardrobe in front of me. A tuft of shirt-sleeve poked out between the doors, entombed.

"So, are you buying anything interesting?" I asked, felt mildly ridiculous.

"Zucchini and Roquefort," she said.

I made a non-committal positive noise that came out of both my nose and my mouth.

"I'm having a dinner party," she said, "hence the dairy."

"I see."

She jabbered on vaguely and quickly, and I wondered if she had clocked that this phone-call was international, the bill mine. Her voice faded in and out as she moved about, paid for things. I heard snippets of music, a dog barking, a child's voice, a paper bag, perhaps, a gentle thud.

I shifted a dust-ball with my toe; pushed it underneath my bed.

"I guess you've picked out your outfit then," I stated, for something to say.

"Oh man," she said, pulling the words out, dragging them along through gravel and grit, "No. I can't decide between a little, black sparkly thing or dress down. Shirt and pants."

"I'd go with pants."

I glanced down to my legs, my underwear.

"Anyway, this isn't why you called," she chuckled.

Then she was talking about her impending trip. She was going to France first, not Paris, but not too far, so maybe she could fit it in, you know? Would be a waste not to see it, after all. And then the train up, but via Caen, as she had a friend there, remember? And then up to the tunnel – how amazing – and England.

"Wow," I said, noting a coffee stain on my bedside cabinet, "sounds exhausting."

She snorted. "You mean exciting!"

"Sure," I laughed softly, "that too."

There was a pause and I could hear her shifting bags. When she spoke again, her voice was clearer, closer to the telephone.

"You still want to meet up?"

I paused, a fraction too long. She would have heard it. One heavy breath came down the phone line to me as a huff of static.

"Of course!" I said, picking a stale crisp from my duvet cover, "I shall wear my best pants."

Broken Eggshells

She returns from shopping on Friday night, grocery bags pulling her fingers into balls of knotted string. The house smells hollow and still. Fusty, with a faint backdrop of lavender; reminds her of her grandmother.

She unpacks her shopping, placing tins in cupboards, fruit in bowls. She leaves the flour, the eggs, the butter, ready to bake a sponge – to evoke her mother through her recipe.

Later, much later, she sleeps well, warm bellied. She sees her, is with her again in vanilla dreams; in jam and hugs and hands holding sticky fingers.

Saturday, and she closes curtains to avoid the sun – she does not need its springtime guilt. Instead, she drinks fragrant tea, watches movies under a blanket, and she remembers him. She remembers him, feels him, and she becomes broken eggshells, skin full of splinters, prickling eyes, buckled, curling inwards, winded - until she can watch no more.

Then Sunday is here, with headaches and quiet, and so she cooks a roast dinner, slowly. Verdant beans. Rich sauce on cauliflower. Meat: strong, scented, heady. She eats for four, at the table, using her father's patterned platter for a plate.

For the rest of the day, she sits in her armchair, and hugs her body with crossed arms. Once an hour she says a word or two aloud; she challenges herself do this. She must.

And on Monday, when they ask - if they do - she will tell faithless truths: of weekends with the family, and sleep, and food. And quiet.

Scarves Like Halos

Running down the steps to the platform. Grey trainers on grey steps in grey air. She isn't sure this is the way. She doesn't know if this is the train. She is scared; she is hopeful.

In her ears, her chest, is a bounding, pounding rhythm. Her quick steps and quick breath mirroring the beat of her blood.

The train is bold and dirty, fierce.

"Excuse me – " she says, but he waves a hand, swats her away like fly, and blows a whistle. The train leaves with a violent sigh.

She sits on a bench and listens to the beat of the air. Listen. She doesn't look around in case she sees them. Why would they be here? Yet they might be. They could be here. People follow you. It's a real thing. They do that.

She has a piece of paper where she has scrawled the timetable and the address. In the corner she has doodled love hearts, pierced. She doesn't know why she did that. Silly. Childish. Yet she pictures the heart as a doodle on her hand, snaking up her wrist, bigger, broader, taking over her skin and turning her pink flesh black. A tattoo.

They'd never expect her to do that.

She should do that.

In front a little, to the left, a young woman stands patiently waiting, hands in the pockets of her black, leather jacket, and a colossal scarf wrapped around her neck, her throat, like a python. The girl's hair rests on the top rung of the scarf, and halos around her face.

'I should do that,' she thinks. 'I should hide in scarves like halos.' No one would recognise her then.

Then the train is here, and they are boarding, her and the girl with the halo. They climb into the same carriage. The girl sits at a table where a man is already settled, reading a paper so large it absorbs the space, tries to take her too. She smiles at the girl, gives a knowing nod, but halo girl slides back, closes her eyes, buries her face inside the mound of hair and wool.

The journey is only 40 minutes. There are some empty seats by windows, which people have claimed with bags, or folded arms, closed faces. She does not bother to fight for them. Her racing blood is abating, but still there, drumming, so to stand would do her good.

Another grey station. More iron-clad roofs, filthy floors, crowds. She takes the stairs, and she runs again; grey shoes, grey steps, dirty fingers, dirty people not looking, but they are watching. They could be. Look. Run.

Then bursting through turnstiles, bleeping and swallowing tickets - and she is outside.

Grey pavement, black sky, chilled air. But all around her, beside and above, there are lights. Neon. Colours. Red; pink; blue. Light trails, snaking, bigger, broader. Primary.

And she knows it for sure, she feels it in her chest, in her blood, her breath.

She is free.

The Funeral

They don't notice me as I slope in the rear of the church. The door is ajar, just a little: I presume they do this for latecomers, like me. Not our job to upset the service. Not for us to be the centre of attention.

I take caterpillar steps on the stone slabs until I reach the back pew.

I thought it would be fuller than this. Services for young people usually are – I should know, I've been to a few. More than I have for the elderly, I realise, and that fact shocks me so much I make a sardonic 'hah!', involuntarily. The woman two rows ahead turns around half-heartedly - to make a point, not to actually look. I place my hands to my disrespectful mouth.

She was a beautiful girl. Shockingly so. That made it worse somehow, that she had died so young, while so lovely - though I know that doesn't make any sense. And hardly fair on the plain ones.

Only twenty-five.

At twenty-five, I was four years into marriage to Thomas, Megan was two. But times are different now. She wasn't married; she hadn't had children. She'd only graduated University three years ago. She had such a lust for travel she'd taken time out between school and College. Backpacking. Volunteering.

That's just how she was.

Her mother is going up to speak now. Startlingly brave. She isn't looking well, clothes and face both crumpled and crinkled, and as she begins her speech, she makes it barely four words in before she is overwhelmed with a wall of pure despair. Horror.

It is harrowing to watch. I reach for my tissues and look away.

I fix my eyes on the image above the altar – a huge poster of her face. A professional shot, I'd guess. She had a gentle smile. Soft. Though it didn't reach her eyes.

And then they are playing some music, and someone reads from a book that I don't know, and before you know it, it's over. It doesn't seem enough really; not enough for a beautiful girl. Twenty-five. Lost.

In three days' time, there is a service for a twenty-one-year-old man, in St Ewold's. I don't usually go to the boys' ones, but am making an exception this time, because he sounds like he is worth it. Training to be a nurse. Doted on his nan. That sort of thing.

I won't be telling Thomas. I tried once; he was furious. Told me I'd get myself in trouble. Told me I was living in the past. Wallowing.

Hah.

Her mother walks past me, glances my way: eyes lost, mouth ajar, haunted, spooked, propped up by a relative. It is a familiar sight. I smile a little smile at her. Try to show I know. She doesn't register it.

He doesn't understand how this is solace for me; that it's the closest I get to being with you again.

A beautiful girl. Shockingly so. Only twenty-five.

This is Where She Died

He lay on the floor and he refused to move. The first four or five minutes had been quite peaceful. The city suits and boots had ignored him. They walked past briskly and regarded him as an inconvenience, but a minor one – if they noticed him at all.

He lay on his back and stared skyward. A Tetris of office blocks rose up, obscuring all but an angular patch of sky. He could hear the swish of acrylic trouser legs; the clatter of high-heels; the mechanics of cars. But he could only see clouds.

No people.

After about five minutes a Police Officer came along and squatted down beside him. This is where she died, he told him. They had a nice little chat before the Officer tugged his arm to get him to his feet. He didn't bother to resist.

The next month he managed only two minutes before a middle-aged woman stopped beside him. He could see her legs, a little ladder in her tights showing a cobweb of white skin beneath. It distracted him from the view above. Irritating.

"What are you doing?" she asked, fiercely.

"This is where she died," he stated.

There was a pause. The legs shuffled slightly, and one foot tapped in time to a little huff from above.

"Don't be so silly," she scolded.

He hadn't expected that. Didn't quite know how to respond, so he ignored her until she went away - and then he left as well.

Month three, and the sky was starting to look a bit more chipper. The little gaps between the high-rise buildings tessellated varying shades of blue and grey together into a new whole. It was quite lovely. But it only lasted around six minutes before a rather concerned looking Doctor came along and squatted down, peering over, obscuring the blues and hues with his weather worn face.

The Doctor kept asking who he could call, and if he was injured, and if he knew his name and the year and had he been drinking and did he need to take any tablets and - until he got up to his feet swiftly, in irritation – or as swiftly as he could, at least - and harrumphed away.

The next month he went an hour earlier, wondering if he might get a longer lie-down if he beat the crowds. The clouds were gone, the sky flat cobalt. Perfect.

Two minutes in – just two minutes - and a young, teenager's voice broke his reverie, damnit.

"Hey mate," she said, quietly. "What you doing?"

At first, he didn't answer, not wanting to be told off again.

"This is where she died," he stated, after it was clear she wasn't going to leave.

"Oh," and then a pause. "Sorry to hear that."

He waited for her to go, or shout, or be worried, but she lay down next to him, on the pavement, and fixed her eyes straight ahead, upwards, to the sky.

"What was her name?" she asked.

Appendix

One Hundred Word Stories

Hitch

He pulled over. I hesitated before lowering my thumb. The car was rusty; engine thudding; water dripped onto the tarmac beneath it.

I got in: seats ripped, innards erupting like a beer-belly over pants.

'Town?' he asked, cheerfully.

'The station, cheers,' I said.

The floor was littered. Apple cores; receipts: I expected him to apologise. He didn't.

I reached for a wallet that lay amongst the debris, while he chattered.

'Hey,' I said, 'anywhere here. Changed my mind about the train.'

I took twenty-pounds - slipped it into his wallet; dropped it again.

'I think I'll hitch,' I said.

Autumn Leaves

My mother boils the kettle in her kitchen. She moves and shakes between surfaces. Her hands are furrowed tree roots; her skin, mottled with liver spots as auburn autumn leaves.

She heaps tea into a pot, cocoons this in a cosy. We stand and wait. A slight tremor jangles her throat.

Three minutes later, maybe four, we march a tray into the lounge.

It is a shy cup of tea, when it comes. Nervous. Pale. Shaking in her hand.

I marvel at her determination, her grace, and I look down; on the surface, specks of loose tea tell our future.

Objects in the Mirror Are Closer Than They Appear

Four of us in the car, where there used to be five. We are shadows of each other, almost reflections. Almost.

Four red-heads, red-freckled faces - a fractal image shifting, wobbling as we travel to the funeral.

He was lying face down when they found him. Fully clothed, belt undone. Swollen belly bursting over denim, over greying pants; can of lager tilted, but gently cradled in his curved palm.

I stare out, into the wing mirror, to picture anything but this.

Four.

Then I swallow hard, take a slow swig from the hip flask cocooned, so gently, between my knees.

I Need to Tell Someone the Truth

I need to tell someone the truth before it's too late... I may burst, stop functioning. The very sound of his voice brings me to life. I can't keep it to myself. I must tell him.

He is home again; I hear steps approaching. The sound of shopping bags, dropping, settling around his feet like a litter of puppies.

Will he speak, acknowledge me? Does he need me, like I need him?

Then he calls to me.

I am plucked as a needle and thread into the air.

'***Siri?***' He says.

'How can I help you, John?' I reply, softly.

The Edge

My demon has stalked me for ninety-two days.

When I awake, he is waiting. Brittle, bird-boned.

By five o'clock, he stands at my desk, close. Bird-boned; rabbit teeth; rabid; wretched. Waiting.

At dusk, I doze, to shut my eyes - push a river of sleep between us. Not much really. Not much to stop him from consuming me whole.

I stand on the edge; wet leaves, lichen, lap at my feet, stick to my legs. He is strong: wants to hold me under - until I am over my head, gulping. Sinking.

Water. Drinking.

Ninety-two days.

Then back to none.

Junk Nest

There's a pair of black pants on the floor of the car. I'm not even shocked. Dad really should be more careful.

Or – you know – loyal.

And how do you forget pants? Little lacy ones, they are. Cobwebs, string.

Sort of forlorn, lost, they look. Tucked, pitifully, under the driver's seat amongst the crisp wrappers and receipts in a nest of junk. Amongst everyday things.

Everyday. Hah! Well, perhaps it is.

Was.

Not anymore.

Come on, little pants. Let's get you out of here. I'll rescue you. Let's take you on another little trip – let me introduce you to mum.

Acknowledgments

Thank you to my readers, both along the way, and of the final product. And to those people who were bombarded with varying book covers before I finally settled on this design (no doubt nothing like ones you had recommended…)

Thank you to the readers and writers of twitter and Instagram, most of whom I have never met, but who are always willing to send words of encouragement. It has made a phenomenal difference to my confidence to have your support.

And, of course, a special thank you to Stuart for his on-going care, love, time and support.

Printed in Great Britain
by Amazon